This
Treasure Cove Story
belongs to

Evie

and Flynn

D0987925

WISH UPON A SLEEPOVER

A CENTUM BOOK 978-1-912396-23-8
Published in Great Britain by Centum Books Ltd.
This edition published 2018. 1 3 5 7 9 10 8 6 4 2

© 2018 Viacom International Inc. All rights reserved. Nickelodeon,
Shimmer & Shine and all related titles, logos and characters
are trademarks of Viacom International Inc.

No part of this publication may be reproduced, stored in a retrieval
system, or transmitted in any form or by any means, electronic,
mechanical, photocopying, recording or otherwise without
the prior permission of the publishers.

Centum Books Ltd, 20 Devon Square, Newton Abbot,
Devon, TQ12 2HR, UK.

www.centumbooksltd.co.uk | books@centumbooksltd.co.uk
CENTUM BOOKS Limited Reg.No. 07641486.

A CIP catalogue record for this book is available
from the British Library.

Printed in China.

centum

A Treasure Cove Story

Adapted by Mary Tillworth
Based on the teleplay 'Sleepover Party' by Lacey Dyer
Illustrated by Liana Hee

nickelodeon

One evening, Shimmer and Shine were getting ready for their first sleepover party with Leah.

'Don't forget the important stuff!' Shine told her sister. 'Like our miner helmet and snorkel – in case Leah wants to go deep-sea gold mining!'

Meanwhile, Leah was putting the finishing touches on her pillow fort. After placing the last pillow, it was time to call the genies!

Leah rubbed her necklace. 'Shimmer and Shine, my genies divine! Through this special chant, three wishes you'll grant!'

Poof! The genies and their pets appeared in Leah's room – right on top of the pillow fort. 'Talk about a soft landing!' laughed Shimmer.

'Welcome to the sleepover party!' said Leah.

In a burst of sparkles, Shimmer and
Shine changed into their pyjamas.

'Now, how does this sleepover thing work?' asked
Shine. 'Do we sleep *over* things, like *over* this bed?'
'Actually, a sleepover is a party where you sleep
at a friend's house,' explained Leah. 'And there's
pizza. And music and dancing!'

'And we get to sleep in a pillow fort!' Leah added. 'Well… we were going to.'

'Don't worry, Leah. We can build a new one!' Shimmer scratched her head. 'Um, what *is* a pillow fort?'

Leah showed the genies how to stack pillows to make a fort. But when they were done, the fort was too small! They needed more pillows.

Shine had an idea – Leah could use her first wish!

'For my first wish,' Leah said, 'I wish for more pillows!'

'Boom, Zahramay! First wish of the day!' chanted Shine.

Suddenly, pillows were everywhere, filling the room from floor to ceiling!

'Is this enough?' Shimmer asked.

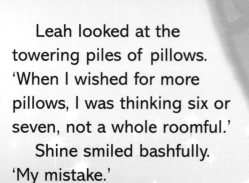

Leah looked at the towering piles of pillows. 'When I wished for more pillows, I was thinking six or seven, not a whole roomful.'

Shine smiled bashfully. 'My mistake.'

'It's okay, Shine. I should have told you how many I wanted.' Leah handed Shine a pillow. 'Now we can try building again.'

Leah concentrated on making a fort. When she
turned around to show the genies, she gasped. 'Whoa!'

Shimmer and Shine had used their magic to turn the whole bedroom into a gigantic pillow fort!

After playing in the fort, Leah and the genies were ready to dance.

Leah tried to put on some tunes, but she discovered that her music player was broken.

'I guess we can't have a dance party after all,' she sighed.

'There's no such thing as *can't* when you still have wishes left!' Shine said with a twinkle in her eye.

'Okay,' Leah said. 'For my second wish, I wish we could play music!'

Shimmer spun her bracelets. *'Boom, Zahramay! Second wish of the day!'*

In a puff of smoke the girls found themselves surrounded by musical instruments!

Leah plucked a guitar string. 'I didn't mean to wish for instruments. I just wanted my music player to work. But maybe we can make our own music for the dance party!'

'A little magic will help us sound perfect.' Shimmer sprinkled pink dust over the instruments. They began to play a rocking beat!

In a shower of blue dust, Shine turned Leah's carpet into a light-up dance floor. The dance party was on!

'This is a blast!' Leah said with a giggle. 'I wish the dancing would never stop!'

Shine clapped her hands. *'Boom, Zahramay! Third wish of the day!'*

Leah laughed as she and the genies strutted around on the dance floor. 'I didn't mean to make that wish, but I love this mistake!'

As the night went on, however, the girls grew tired. 'We need to stop dancing, but there are no wishes left!' said Leah.

Shine was pooped, too. 'Even my ears are tired,'
she said, picking up a pillow. 'I'm going to give them
a rest.' She held a pillow over each ear and the sound
of music faded away.

'Shine, you've stopped dancing!' exclaimed Leah.

That gave Leah an idea! She reached for a pillow and threw it onto the drums. 'Everybody pile the pillows on the instruments!'

The genies and their pets tossed pillows left and right. With a magical wave, Shimmer collapsed the pillow fort onto the instruments. The music stopped and so did the dancing!

Leah hugged the two genies. 'We fixed our mistakes, and the night turned out great!'

Shine yawned. 'And now it's time to get some *sleep* at this sleepover!'

Treasure Cove Stories

Book list may be subject to change.

An ongoing series to collect and enjoy!